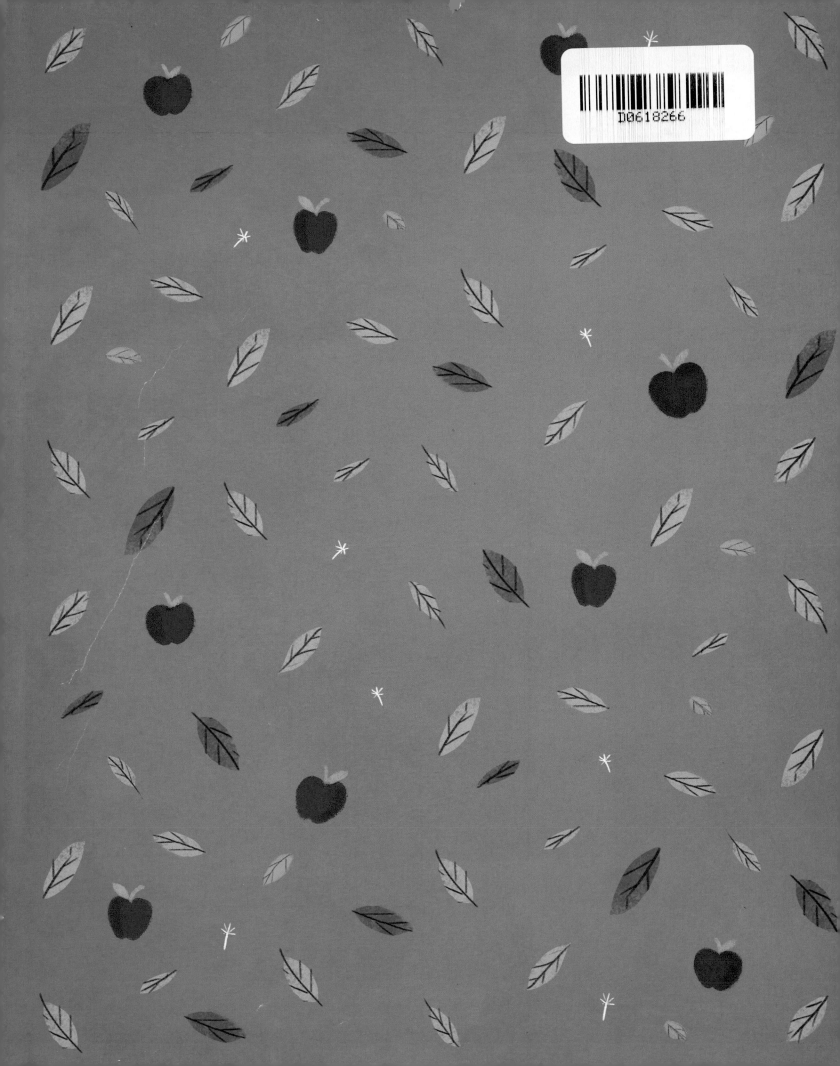

For my mum
and for my late, great, Aussie grandmother,
Gwen "Mate" Hearnshaw —E. W.

In memory of Evelyn and Wyn,
my two lovely grandmas —S. L.

Henry Holt and Company, *Publishers since 1866*
Henry Holt® is a registered trademark of Macmillan Publishing Group, LLC
175 Fifth Avenue, New York, NY 10010 · mackids.com

Text copyright © 2017 by Elli Woollard
Illustrations copyright © 2017 by Steven Lenton
All rights reserved.

Library of Congress Control Number: 2018955696
ISBN 978-1-250-18603-4

Our books may be purchased in bulk for promotional, educational, or business use.
Please contact your local bookseller or the Macmillan Corporate and Premium Sales Department
at (800) 221-7945 ext. 5442 or by email at MacmillanSpecialMarkets@macmillan.com.

First published in the United Kingdom by Macmillan UK, 2017
First American edition, 2019

Printed in China by Shenzhen Wing King Tong Paper Products Co Ltd,
Guangdong Province
1 3 5 7 9 10 8 6 4 2

The Great Gran Plan

Elli Woollard

Steven Lenton

GODWIN BOOKS

Henry Holt and Company

New York

The pig had a house in the Wild Wild Wood.
It was safe, it was strong, it was snug, it was good!

So when the bad wolf started howling and prowling
and skulking and scowling and grizzling and growling,

the pig said, "Old wolf, you can blow till you're blue!
But you'll not break my house down, whatever you do."

The wolf simply glared, then slunk slowly away.
But there, on the pathway, the very next day,
the pig found a note that said . . .

TOP SECRET PLOT

1. ~~Eat the Three Little Pigs~~

2. Gobble Red Riding Hood's gran nice and hot!

"No!" cried the pig. "Oh, my trusty old trotter!
That stinky old fleabag, that wily old rotter!"
And he leaped to the wheel of his rusty old van,
crying, "Pig to the rescue—

SAVE THAT GRAN!"

P1G E

GIANT! SALE!

"I'll snatch him, I'll catch him,
that wolf won't escape!
But first what I need is a Superpig cape."

WIZARD WEAR

APPLE STALL

Staffs Wanted

So he
dashed
through the
town till he
came to a stall.
They hadn't a cape . . .

Wanda's Wands

. . . but they gave him a shawl.

Then he leaped to the wheel of his rusty old van,
crying, "Pig to the rescue—

SAVE THAT GRAN!"

"Now, I'll have to be sneaky. I might have to spy.
Binoculars! Yes! I should give them a try."

So he dashed to the shop, and there weren't any there!

But he did find some rather fine specs (the last pair).

Then he leaped to the wheel of his rusty old van,
crying, "Pig to the rescue—

SAVE THAT GRAN!"

"I'll swoop on that wolfie. I'll hoop him, I hope.
But now what I need is some lovely strong rope."
So he dashed to the city; the shops were so full!

Emporium of New Clothes

ROPE-UNZEL'S

Peep's BO-tique

OPEN ALL KNIGHT

And the rope was sold out . . .

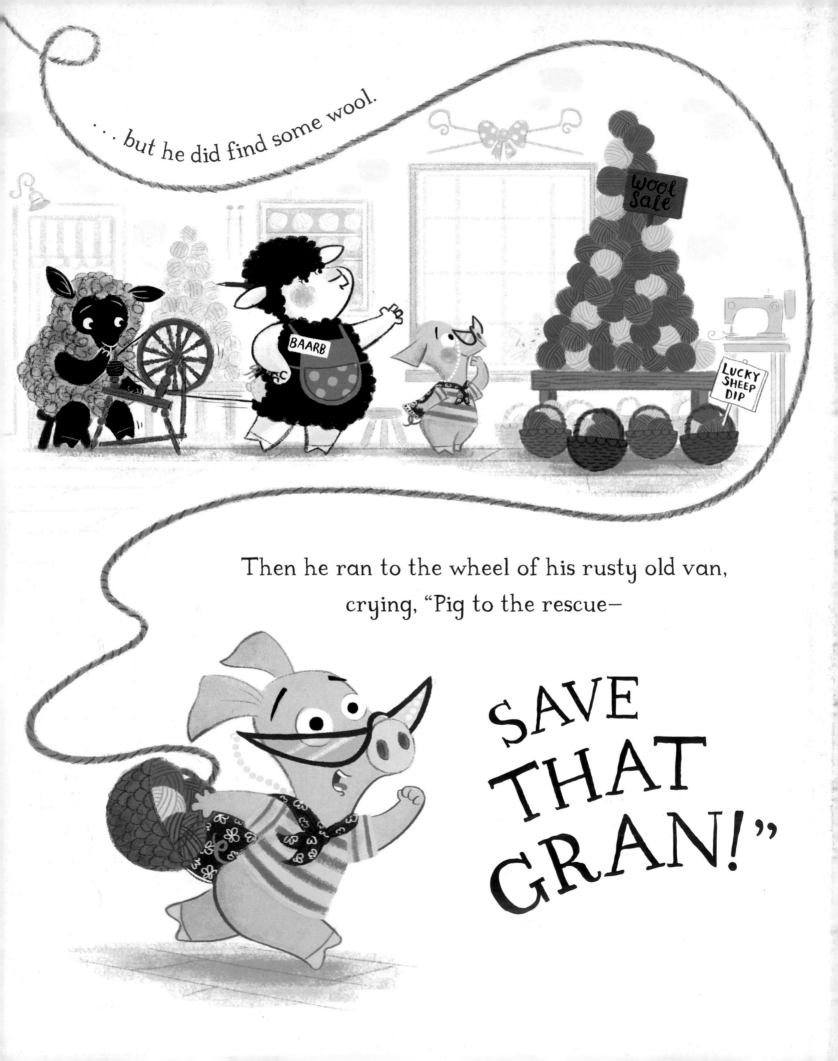

. . . but he did find some wool.

Then he ran to the wheel of his rusty old van,
crying, "Pig to the rescue—

SAVE
THAT
GRAN!"

But just as he came to the edge of the wood,
he stopped most abruptly . . .

. . . as there the wolf stood!

"Red Riding Hood's granny? Well, how do you do?
Strangely enough, I've been searching for you.
Although, I admit that it's quite a surprise!
You've such a strange nose and such small piggy eyes."

Gran? thought the pig, and he took a long look . . .

Then he quivered and quaked, and he shivered and shook.

The wolf eyed him up and snarled, "Mmm, nice and plump!
Not old and not chewy—just look at that rump!
You'd taste rather rare in a roll, I would bet."
And he lunged at the pig, but then . . .

. . . down came a net!

And there, in the wood, was Red Riding Hood's gran,
who cried, "Think we can't catch you?

YOU BET
THAT WE
CAN!"

"You wicked old wolf. You may huff, you may puff.
But I'm telling you now, I have had quite ENOUGH!"

Then she tied up the wolf from his nose to his tail.
And together they took him and dropped him in jail.

FAIRY-TALE
JAIL

"Thanks!" cried the pig, but the gran said, "Thank *you*! That wolf would have minced me for gray granny stew!"

And linking together, they danced out a jig, the wolf-busting gran and the clever young pig.

And the wolf never came there again . . .

fairy-tale fete

"Yes!" they both said.
"We're an excellent team!"

. . . it would seem.